12/17
Eleanor
Love: Dalley, Taylor
Ruby, Pearl and Shep

GREG PIZZOLI

For Dad

All rights reserved. Published by Disney • Hyperion, an imprint of Disney Book Group.
No part of this book may be reproduced or transmitted in any form or by any means,
electronic or mechanical, including photocopying, recording, or by any information
storage and retrieval system, without written permission from the publisher.
For information address Disney • Hyperion, 125 West End Avenue, New York, New York 10023.

First Edition, September 2017

10 9 8 7 6 5 4 3 2 1
FAC-029191-17167
Printed in Malaysia
Illustrations were created in silkscreen and digital collage

Library of Congress Cataloging-in-Publication Data

Names: Pizzoli, Greg, author.
Title: The twelve days of Christmas / Greg Pizzoli.
Other titles: Twelve days of Christmas (English folk song)
Description: First edition. Los Angeles ; New York : Disney Hyperion, 2017.
Summary: An elephant parent has to take responsibility for caring for all of the gifts
that arrive in this newly illustrated version of the traditional song.
Identifiers: LCCN 2016032327 ISBN 9781484750315 (hardcover)
ISBN 1484750314 (hardcover)
Subjects: LCSH: Folk songs, English—Texts. Christmas music—Texts
CYAC: Folk songs—England. Christmas music.
Classification: LCC PZ8.3.P558687 Twe 2017 DDC 782.42/1723 [E]—dc23
LC record available at https://lccn.loc.gov/2016032327

Reinforced binding

Visit www.DisneyBooks.com

THE 12 DAYS OF CHRISTMAS

GREG PIZZOLI

Disⁿey · HYPERION ✳ Los Angeles ✳ New York

On the **FIRST** day of Christmas,
my true love gave to me . . .

A partridge in a pear tree.

On the **SECOND** day of Christmas,
my true love gave to me . . .

Two turtle doves,
And a partridge in a pear tree.

On the **THIRD** day of Christmas,
my true love gave to me . . .

Three French hens,
Two turtle doves,
And a partridge in a pear tree.

On the **FOURTH** day of Christmas,
my true love gave to me . . .

Four calling birds,
Three French hens,
Two turtle doves,
And a partridge in a pear tree.

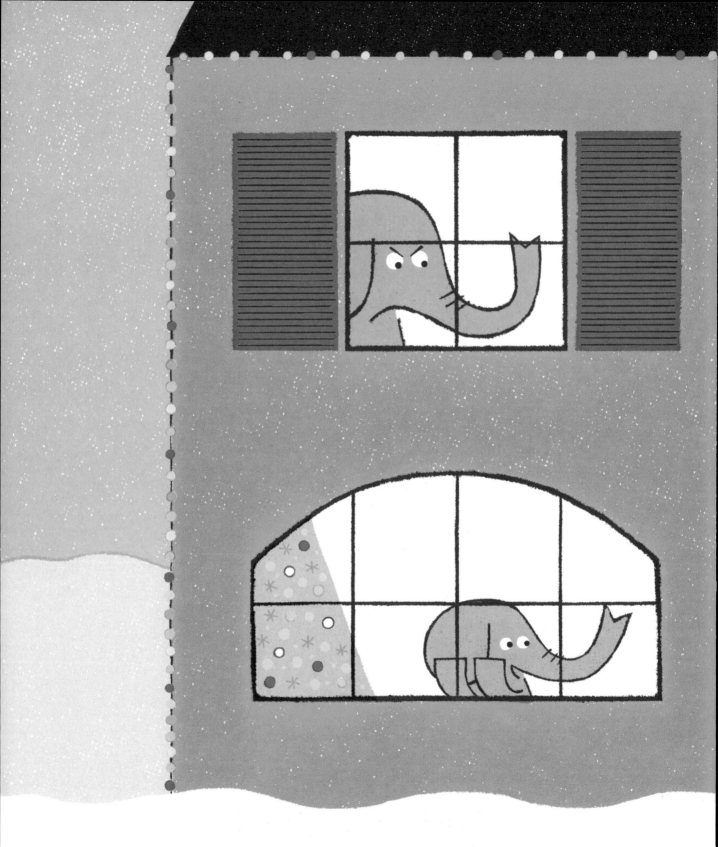

On the **FIFTH** day of Christmas,

my true love gave to me . . .

Five golden rings,

Four calling birds,
Three French hens,
Two turtle doves,
And a partridge in a pear tree.

PHEW!

BULK BIRDSEED

On the **SIXTH** day of Christmas,
my true love gave to me . . .

Six geese a-laying,
Five golden rings,
Four calling birds,
Three French hens,
Two turtle doves,
And a partridge in a pear tree.

On the **SEVENTH** day of Christmas,
my true love gave to me . . .

Seven swans a-swimming,
Six geese a-laying,
Five golden rings,
Four calling birds,
Three French hens,
Two turtle doves,
And a partridge in a pear tree.

On the **EIGHTH** day of Christmas,
my true love gave to me . . .

Eight maids a-milking,
Seven swans a-swimming,
Six geese a-laying,
Five golden rings,
Four calling birds,
Three French hens,
Two turtle doves,
And a partridge in a pear tree.

On the **NINTH** day of Christmas,
my true love gave to me . . .

Nine ladies dancing,
Eight maids a-milking,
Seven swans a-swimming,
Six geese a-laying,
Five golden rings,
Four calling birds,
Three French hens,
Two turtle doves,
And a partridge in a pear tree.

On the **TENTH** day of Christmas,
my true love gave to me . . .

Ten lords a-leaping,
Nine ladies dancing,
Eight maids a-milking,
Seven swans a-swimming,
Six geese a-laying,
Five golden rings,
Four calling birds,
Three French hens,
Two turtle doves,
And a partridge
in a pear tree.

On the **ELEVENTH** day of Christmas,
my true love gave to me . . .

Eleven pipers piping,
Ten lords a-leaping,
Nine ladies dancing,
Eight maids a-milking,
Seven swans a-swimming,
Six geese a-laying,
Five golden rings,
Four calling birds,
Three French hens,
Two turtle doves,
And a partridge in a pear tree.

On the TWELFTH day of Christmas,
my true love gave to me . . .

12 DRUMMERS DRUMMING

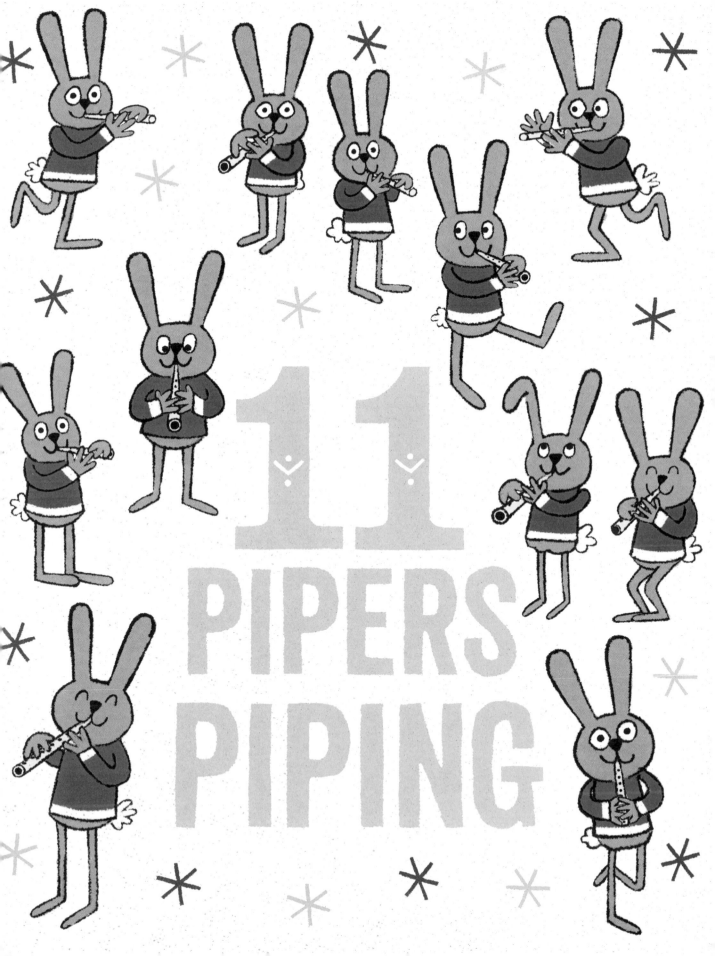

10 LORDS A-LEAPING

9 LADIES DANCING

8 MAIDS A-MILKING

7 SWANS A-SWIMMING

6 GEESE A-LAYING

5 GOLDEN RINGS

3 FRENCH HENS

2 TURTLE DOVES

And a partridge in a pear tree!